A Note to Par

DK READERS is a compelling progran
readers, designed in conjunction with leading literacy
experts, including Maureen Fernandes, B.Ed (Hons).
Maureen has spent many years teaching literacy, both in the
classroom and as a consultant in schools.

Beautiful illustrations and superb full-colour photographs
combine with engaging, easy-to-read stories to offer a fresh
approach to each subject in the series. Each DK READER is
guaranteed to capture a child's interest while developing his
or her reading skills, general knowledge and love of reading.

The five levels of DK READERS are aimed at different
reading abilities, enabling you to choose the books that are
exactly right for your child:

Pre-level 1: Learning to read

Level 1: Beginning to read

Level 2: Beginning to read alone

Level 3: Reading alone

Level 4: Proficient readers

The "normal" age at which a child
begins to read can be anywhere from
three to eight years old. Adult
participation through the lower levels
is very helpful for providing
encouragement, discussing storylines
and sounding out unfamiliar words.

No matter which level you select, you can be
sure that you are helping your child learn to
read, then read to learn!

Penguin
Random
House

For DK
Senior Editor Laura Gilbert
Senior Designer David McDonald
Designers Sandra Perry,
Stefan Georgiou
Production Controller Sara Hu
Pre-Production Producer Siu Chan
Managing Editor Sadie Smith
Design Managers Guy Harvey,
Ron Stobbart
Creative Manager Sarah Harland
Art Director Lisa Lanzarini
Publisher Julie Ferris
Publishing Director Simon Beecroft

Reading Consultant
Maureen Fernandes

This edition published in 2017
First published in Great Britain in 2010 by
Dorling Kindersley Limited,
80 Strand, London, WC2R 0RL
A Penguin Random House Company

015-176236-Apr/2010

marvel.com
© 2017 MARVEL

A CIP catalogue record for this book is available from
the British Library.

ISBN 978-1-4053-5093-8

Printed and bound in China

www.dk.com

A WORLD OF IDEAS:
SEE ALL THERE IS TO KNOW

Contents

DK READERS

MARVEL
IRON MAN

PROFICIENT
4
READERS

THE RISE OF
IRON MAN

Written by Michael Teitelbaum

Introduction

Tony Stark is a scientific genius, an amazing inventor, a brilliant businessman and one of the richest men in the world. He is also the armour-clad Super Hero known as Iron Man.

It was clear from an early age that Tony was a genius. When he was seven years old, his wealthy parents sent him off to a boarding school. However, he was more interested in machines and how they worked than in making friends with the other children. By the time he was 15, Tony had been accepted at one of the best colleges in America. Four years later, he graduated at the top of his class. When Tony was 21, his parents were tragically killed in a car crash. Tony inherited their company called Stark Industries.

Business mind
Young Tony was not really interested in the family company. However, when he took over Stark Industries, he proved himself to be highly skilled in the world of business.

Great inventor
Tony is always
busy inventing
new gadgets
or improving
old ones.

Stark Industries is a large company
that makes weapons for the military.
Even as head of Stark Industries,
Tony preferred his laboratory to the
boardroom and continued to invent
new things. One invention would
change Tony's life forever.

After hours
At the end of
a busy day,
Tony likes to go
out to cool
nightclubs.

Large and small
Tony's inventions range from large items, like this aircraft carrier, to small things, such as a holo-communicator wristwatch that projects holograms.

Stark the inventor

The Starkworld Tech Conference takes place every year. Fans of the latest gadgets and computers attend this meeting. Each year, Tony reveals his latest invention.

One year, Tony unveiled a glider made of the lightest, sturdiest substance ever created. The substance is called Synth-Kinetic Interface Nano-fluid (S.K.I.N.).

The S.K.I.N. glider was powered by thermal uplifts and solar energy. Tony claimed that he would be the first person to fly around the Earth using powerless flight.

At the conference, inventor Dr Ho Yinsen accused Tony of making weapons that had destroyed the country of Madripoor. Tony denied it, but Ho Yinsen's words upset him.

Tony took off in his glider, but a tornado threw the plane around and sent Tony crashing to the ground.

Dr Ho Yinsen
Dr Ho Yinsen was a brilliant and respected physicist, engineer and professor. He did not believe in war and was against producing weapons.

Iron Man rising

When Tony awoke, he had been taken prisoner by agents of A.I.M. (Advanced Idea Mechanics). Tony learned that A.I.M. had been buying his company's weapons and using them to destroy Madripoor.

Tony was thrown into a high-tech lab filled with weapons and the remains of his S.K.I.N. glider. A.I.M. ordered him to build them an arsenal of weapons. They provided him with help – Dr Yinsen himself, whom they had also kidnapped.

In secret, Tony and Yinsen used the S.K.I.N. material from the plane to build two suits of armour. They added weapons then donned the suits and blasted their way out. Yinsen did not survive, but Tony did and Iron Man was born.

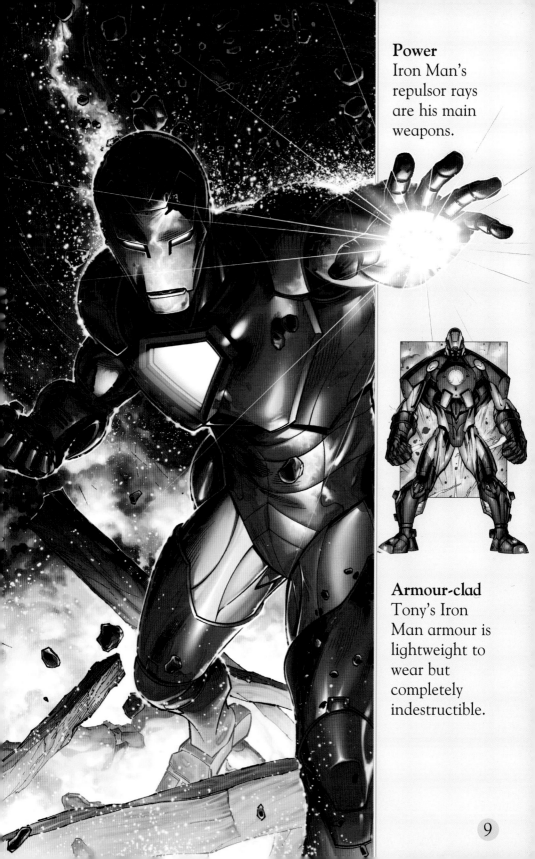

Power
Iron Man's repulsor rays are his main weapons.

Armour-clad
Tony's Iron Man armour is lightweight to wear but completely indestructible.

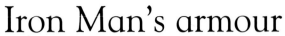

Iron Man's armour

The original armour Tony built, while a prisoner of A.I.M., was just the first step in the development of the Iron Man battlesuit.

Back in his laboratory, Tony perfected the suit, and added several new weapons and features. Over many years of battling different Super Villains as Iron Man, Tony was able to develop a number of different types of armour. Each suit was designed for a special use, but all of the suits had elements in common.

The suit
Iron Man's armour protects him from attack and hides his true identity.

10

All of the suits are made of very strong but highly flexible materials. They all contain various weapons and a force field for added protection. Every suit gives Iron Man increased strength, the ability to fly and a radar and communications system. Each suit contains a unibeam in the chest that acts as a spotlight as well as a laser, repulsor rays in the gloves and jet boots.

Weapons
As well as his repulsor rays, Iron Man has a unibeam in his chest that can fire blasts.

Jet boots
The jet boots in Iron Man's armour allow him to fly at great speeds.

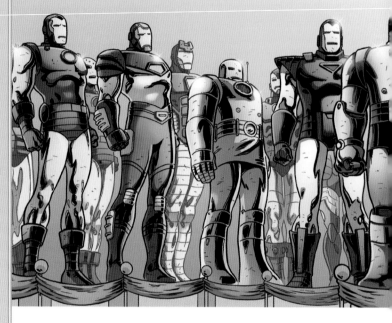

Specialized armour

Many of Iron Man's suits were built
to cope with special situations or to
battle specific beings.

The space armour is extra
strong to stand up to the
pressures of operating in deep
space. It has solar collectors to
harness the sun's energy, and food
and oxygen sources. It also has an
external thruster to help Iron
Man break free of Earth's
gravitational pull.

Iron Man's undersea armour is leakproof and allows Iron Man to remain at the bottom of the ocean for long periods. Its weapons include manta ray torpedoes, an ink cloud like a squid's, and an electric field similar to an electric eel's.

Iron Man also created the Hulkbuster armour to fight the Hulk.

Undersea armour
Iron Man's regular armour can operate underwater for short periods of time, but his underwater suit is better for longer missions.

Hulkbuster armour
The Hulkbuster armour features enhanced strength and a very strong shell.

Tony's allies

As a businessman, Tony relies on his loyal friends.

Harold "Happy" Hogan was an unsuccessful boxer. When Tony was in a crash at a stock-car race, Hogan saved his life. A grateful Tony made Hogan his chauffeur.

Virginia "Pepper" Potts works at Stark Industries. When she corrected an error Tony had made, Tony made her his assistant. The pair care for each other, but their work relationship comes first.

Iron Man zooms in to rescue his loyal friends Happy Hogan and Pepper Potts.

Happy and Pepper
Both Happy and Pepper worked for Stark Industries. They soon fell in love with each other and married.

RHODES

James "Rhodey" Rhodes is Tony's pilot and trusted ally. He wore Iron Man's armour and filled in for Tony when Tony had personal problems. He has also battled various Super Villains while wearing the War Machine armour.

Edwin Jarvis is Tony's butler and has been with the Stark family for several years. When the Stark mansion became the Avengers' headquarters, Jarvis became butler to the Super Hero team and remained loyal to all its members.

Rhodey
Tony and Rhodey met when Rhodey was a pilot in the military.

Edwin Jarvis
Jarvis was a pilot during World War II. After the war, he went to work as a butler for Tony's parents, Howard and Maria Stark, at their mansion.

Iron Man's allies

Iron Man has teamed up with many Super Heroes, both on his own and as a member of the Super Hero group the Avengers.

The Hulk is a member of the Avengers and one of the strongest beings on Earth. The Hulk was created by a gamma ray blast and is a green mountain of muscle. Iron Man has also fought the Hulk a few times, using his Hulkbuster armour.

The Hulk and Spider-Man
Both these heroes have teamed up with Iron Man many times, but they have also battled him.

Thor and Captain America
Thor and Captain America team up with Iron Man to make a tough trio.

Captain America is another of Iron Man's teammates in the Avengers. He was transformed to the peak of human perfection by a top secret Super-Soldier Serum. With Iron Man, he fights against Super Villains, alien invaders and terrorists.

Nick Fury
Nick Fury is the director of S.H.I.E.L.D., a major anti-terrorist group. Iron Man helps Fury to work with Super Heroes.

Mandarin
A blast from one of Mandarin's rings can slam into Iron Man's unibeam.

Ten Rings
Each of Mandarin's Ten Rings has a different power.

Iron Man's enemies

Both Tony and Iron Man have had to battle some tough enemies over the years.

Mandarin is a superpowered martial arts master and one of Iron Man's greatest enemies. Mandarin wears the Ten Rings of Power. They respond to his commands and allow him to seize control of another being's mind, rearrange matter and create fire, ice, electricity and blinding bursts of light.

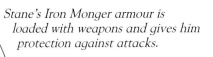

Stane's Iron Monger armour is loaded with weapons and gives him protection against attacks.

Tony's greatest foe is Obadiah Stane, a brilliant but ruthless businessman who tried to ruin Tony and take over Stark Industries. Stane also fought Iron Man as the armoured Iron Monger.

Financial genius Justin Hammer tried to take over Tony's company. He used a high-tech device to gain control of Iron Man's armour. When Hammer used the armour to kill an ambassador, Iron Man was blamed, but Tony cleared his name.

Further foes

Iron Man has battled with several other dangerous Super Villains over the years.

The Crimson Dynamo wears a battlesuit similar to Iron Man's own. This suit is loaded with weapons, from missiles to guns, to electric blast generators. Many enemies, such as Crimson Dynamo, have attempted to destroy Iron Man using this type of technology. All of them have failed.

Doctor Doom
Victor von Doom is a great scientist. As the Super Villain Doctor Doom, he is a dangerous foe to Iron Man.

Crimson Dynamo

Backlash

Originally, Backlash was called Whiplash. He wore a battlesuit of steel mesh and a bulletproof cape. Justin Hammer later provided him with new weapons and armour, and he became Backlash.

Ultimo is a giant robot created by an alien race. The android was reprogrammed by Mandarin. Ultimo's aim is to destroy Iron Man. The two have fought many battles.

Titanium Man also wears armour like Iron Man's. His suit protects him from attacks, allows him to fly and lets him fire energy blasts.

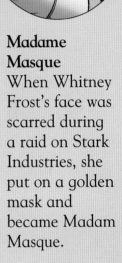

Madame Masque
When Whitney Frost's face was scarred during a raid on Stark Industries, she put on a golden mask and became Madam Masque.

Ultimo

Titanium Man

Tony's loves

Tony has been in love on several occasions. Some of his girlfriends have worked for him at Stark Industries. Others started as Iron Man's enemies but switched sides later. All of them have one thing in common: they loved the billionaire businessman who became an armoured Super Hero.

Bethany Cabe went to work for Tony as his bodyguard. She quickly fell in love with him. Bethany had been married before, but she believed that her husband had been killed in a car accident. She was shocked to find that her husband was still alive. Bethany promptly left Tony to help her husband. A faithful friend, she later returned to nurse Tony back to health when his personal problems became too much for him.

Natasha Romanova was a Russian spy who used the code name "Black Widow". She hoped to steal Tony's technological secrets for the Russians. Hawkeye, a member of the Avengers, convinced Black Widow to change sides to America. Instead of stealing from Tony, she fell in love with him.

Black Widow
Black Widow is an expert at martial arts and a weapons specialist. Before she got her costume, she performed her spy missions in evening wear.

Maya Hansen
Scientist Maya Hansen was Tony's longtime friend. However, she betrayed Iron Man by letting her dangerous Extremis formula get into the hands of terrorists.

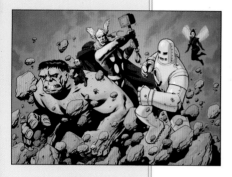

The Avengers

The Avengers is a Super Hero team whose line-up has changed over the years. Through the changes, Iron Man has remained one of the Avengers' staunchest supporters and even its leader at times.

Iron Man never meant to be in a team. However, when the evil Loki tried to trick the Hulk into causing a train crash, Iron Man joined with Thor, Ant-Man and Wasp.

Line-up
In addition to well-known heroes, the Avengers has consisted of supernatural beings, humans, robots and aliens.

Loki
Loki cannot read the minds of others, but he can control their actions.

The heroes decided to stop the Hulk. When they realized that Loki had tricked them, they came together to stop him. Ant-Man suggested they remain a team and Wasp came up with the name. The Avengers was born.

Tony's money and technical genius, the equipment and resources of Stark Industries and the power of Iron Man have all helped to keep the team going.

Other Avengers
Over the years other members of the Avengers team have included Ronin, Luke Cage, Spider-Woman, Sentry, Spider-Man, Wolverine and Captain America.

The Avengers battle superhuman and alien threats wherever they appear.

Director of S.H.I.E.L.D.
Nick Fury's combat experience and his Super Hero contacts made him the perfect choice to be the Director of S.H.I.E.L.D.

S.H.I.E.L.D.

S.H.I.E.L.D. stands for Supreme Headquarters International Espionage Law-enforcement Division. This anti-terrorism organization often needs help from Iron Man and the Avengers.

S.H.I.E.L.D. was formed mainly to deal with threats from superhumans. It was set up by the US government.

World War II commando Nick Fury was selected to lead the highly skilled and well-armed group of S.H.I.E.L.D. agents. Captain America, Spider-Woman and Iron Man have all served as S.H.I.E.L.D. agents, and the entire Avengers team is often called on to assist the organization. Fury has also had to ask for help from other Super Heroes, like the Fantastic Four, on more than one occasion.

Headquarters
S.H.I.E.L.D.'s base is on a huge aircraft called the Helicarrier. It was created by Stark Industries.

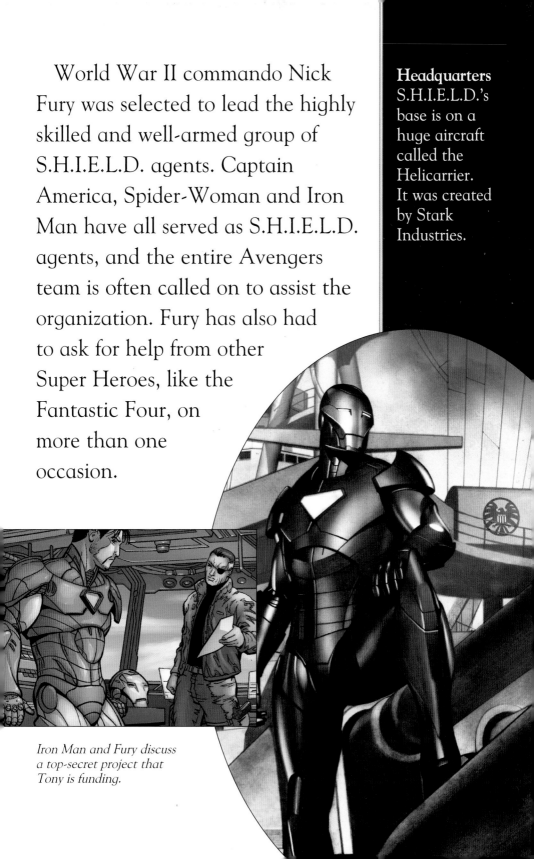

Iron Man and Fury discuss a top-secret project that Tony is funding.

A new Iron Man

It seems that Tony has a perfect life.
He is a rich businessman, and, as
Iron Man, he is a powerful Super
Hero. However, Tony has many foes
who envy him and want to ruin him.

Iron Man had always
supported S.H.I.E.L.D. until
he found out the agency was
secretly buying parts of Stark
Industries. The group hoped to
take over Stark Industries and
get the company to make
weapons just for the group.

At the same time, Obadiah Stane tricked Tony into losing control of Stark Industries. Devastated, Tony was unable to act as Iron Man.

Luckily, Tony's close friend James Rhodes was around to help. Rhodey put on the Iron Man armour and took his friend's place. Tony started to put his life back together, but

Rhodey began to go mad. Tony realized that Rhodey could not use the armour for very long because it was designed for Tony. Tony used a magnetic lock to shut down the armour and save his friend.

Armoured friend
Rhodey's War Machine armour is solar-charged. Like Iron Man's armour, it has a powerful unibeam.

Scarlet Witch
Scarlet Witch is a member of the Avengers and Force Works. She has incredible mental powers.

Spider-Woman
Spider-Woman can stick to walls, has great strength and can fly.

Force Works

Iron Man decided to leave the Avengers just as another Super Hero team called the West Coast Avengers split up.

Iron Man joined up with some of the former West Coast Avengers to form a new group, which he called Force Works.

The other members of this new team were Scarlet Witch, US Agent, Wonder Man and Spider-Woman. An alien called Century and War Machine also joined the group, but soon left when they came into conflict with Iron Man.

Force Works battled many aliens, such as the Kree.

The team also had adventures around the world. Eventually the group split up. The members went their separate ways and Iron Man returned to the Avengers.

US Agent
US Agent has superhuman strength.
He carries an indestructible shield made of Vibranium.

Wonder Man
Wonder Man is as strong as Thor. He flies using a jet flight-pack.

Kang the Conqueror
Kang battled Iron Man and the Avengers right from the team's formation.

Death and rebirth

For several years, the time traveller Kang the Conqueror controlled Tony's mind. Kang forced Iron Man to kill many individuals, including some of his Avengers teammates.

The remaining Avengers travelled back in time. They recruited a young Tony to return with them and fight the adult Tony and Kang.

Stealing a suit of Tony's Iron Man armour, teenage Tony engaged in battle with adult Tony. During this struggle, adult Tony remembered all the individuals who he had been forced to kill and broke free of Kang's mind control. Tony destroyed Kang and sacrificed himself in the battle.

One Iron Man battling another Iron Man means double the trouble!

Teen Tony stayed in the present and teamed up with the Avengers to battle the evil mutant Onslaught. During this battle, teen Tony was killed, along with his fellow Avengers and the Fantastic Four. Fortunately, Franklin Richards, son of Sue and Reed Richards from the Fantastic Four, had created a pocket universe, which was used to restore adult Tony's life and the life of the other heroes.

Onslaught
Onslaught was formed when Professor X's and Magneto's minds clashed. It has Professor X's mental skills and Magneto's magnetic powers.

Franklin Richards held the key to saving the lives of the Avengers.

Ultron
Ultron was built as a servant but this superpowered robot gained a mind of its own.

Stark versus Iron Man

Tony's Iron Man armour has always been his most valuable tool. But what if the armour came alive and had a mind of its own? This is exactly what happened!

Tony tried to save an android by downloading its programming into his Iron Man suit. However, he did not know that the evil robot Ultron had embedded himself in the android's system. As a result, when the Super Villain Whiplash sent a shock into the Iron Man armour, Tony suffered a heart attack.

That shock also awakened the armour and gave it a mind of its own.

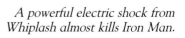

A powerful electric shock from Whiplash almost kills Iron Man.

When his battlesuit comes alive, Iron Man is forced to fight himself.

The armour realized that Tony had suffered a heart attack. It ripped out some of its own parts and built a cybernetic heart that saved Tony's life. However, when the armour tried to force Tony to merge with it, he knew he had to fight it.

The human Tony had no chance of defeating the powerful armour he had built. During the fight, Tony suffered another heart attack. This time the armour decided to save Tony's life by sacrificing itself.

Whiplash
Whiplash wears a bulletproof cape and is an expert at martial arts and hand-to-hand combat.

Tony watches in amazement as his Iron Man armour is ruined.

35

Scarlet Witch
This mutant went insane when she lost her children. She believed the Avengers were to blame.

Avengers disassembled

"Avengers assemble" is the battle cry used to gather the Avengers team together. However, when the Scarlet Witch went insane, the team was forced to disassemble.

The Scarlet Witch is a mutant who can alter reality. Usually the Scarlet Witch can control this power, but when she went insane, she lost control. She manipulated Tony into saying that the country of Latveria should be destroyed.

Tony then announced that the Avengers were breaking up. He knew that people did not trust him because of his remarks about Latveria. He said that someone else would be wearing his armour. Tony hoped this would stop people from mistrusting Iron Man. However, he secretly continued to be Iron Man.

A new group of Super Heroes came together to continue the Avengers' work. This team is called the New Avengers.

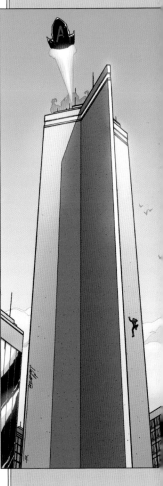

The New Avengers, including Spider-Man, Spider-Woman and Wolverine, burst into action.

Stark Tower
When the Scarlet Witch destroyed the Avengers' mansion, Tony built Stark Tower. This became the New Avengers' base.

37

Professor X
Professor Charles Xavier is a mutant with incredible mental powers. He fights for mutant-human equality and cooperation.

Doctor Strange
Doctor Strange can probe the minds of others and has a cloak of levitation that allows him to fly.

The Illuminati

Following the long war between the alien races known as the Kree and the Skrulls, Iron Man decided to form a new secret organization called the Illuminati. He hoped that the combined knowledge and abilities of the team's members would be able to prevent wars in the future.

Iron Man brought together some of the most important Super Heroes. Each member represented a different group of individuals.

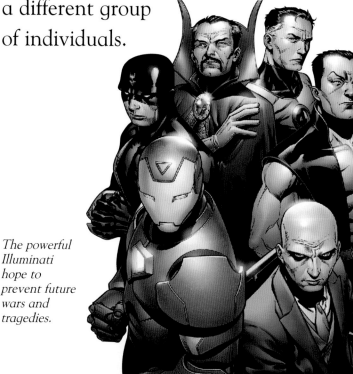

The powerful Illuminati hope to prevent future wars and tragedies.

Iron Man represented the government. Mr. Fantastic stood for the scientific community while Prince Namor, the Sub-Mariner, represented the seas. Professor X, the leader of the X-Men, was the representative of the mutant community, and Black Bolt stood for the Inhumans. Doctor Strange, Master of the Mystic Arts, represented the magical community.

However, the Illuminati became divided because some members started to distrust each other. Ultimately, the Illuminati split up.

When Prince Namor disagreed with the Illuminati, Iron Man tried to convince him otherwise. The pair ended up fighting over it.

Black Bolt
This Inhuman can trigger shock waves, create force fields and has superhuman strength.

Mr. Fantastic
Mr. Fantastic is a scientist and can stretch his body. He got his powers from cosmic radiation.

39

Civil war

The American government had been considering passing an act called the Superhuman Registration Act. This would mean that every superhuman would have to register with the government. The debate over this act would lead to a civil war among the Super Heroes.

Some heroes were for the act while others were against it. At first, Iron Man was unhappy with it. He believed it would take away superhumans' privacy.

Nitro
Nitro can cause his body to explode, then can reform it at will.

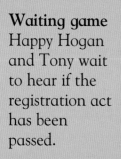

Waiting game
Happy Hogan and Tony wait to hear if the registration act has been passed.

Iron Man's view changed when members of a Super Hero team called the New Warriors confronted Super Villain Nitro in a crowded neighbourhood. The battle ended when Nitro caused a massive explosion. Many innocent people died. From this point on, Iron Man was in favour of the registration act.

The act was passed but the Super Heroes were still divided about the issue. The two sides battled in a civil war. The Super Heroes who had fought alongside each other were now fighting against each other.

New Warriors
The New Warriors do not always see eye to eye with Iron Man.

Brutal battle
The civil war saw Super Hero fight Super Hero. Even Captain America and Iron Man clashed during the huge conflict.

World war Hulk

The Illuminati were concerned about the Hulk. They believed that the Hulk's outbursts were a threat to the safety of Earth. So, Iron Man and the team tricked the Hulk into entering a spaceship and launched it to another planet.

Blasted off!
The Illuminati agreed that the only way to save Earth from the Hulk was to blast him into space.

Some time later, the Hulk returned to Earth and vowed to get his revenge on the Illuminati. Iron Man was the first hero to confront the angry Hulk. Tony realized his armour would not stand up to the Hulk.

When Iron Man donned his Hulkbuster armour, the Hulk put on some new armour of his own.

Hulkbuster armour
Tony created the new Hulkbuster armour. It is a shell that fits around Iron Man's normal armour. The gloves are rocket-boosted and can hit the Hulk with a mighty punch.

Instead, he put on special Hulkbuster armour.

However, Iron Man's new armour was no match for the power of the Hulk and the Hulk destroyed the armour. Iron Man fought back and used a satellite to hit Hulk with a gamma blast, which knocked him unconscious and ended the battle.

Battle damage
The huge fight between the Hulk and Iron Man ruined the city. Even Stark Tower was destroyed.

Secret invasion

In the world of Super Heroes and Villains, it is not always easy to tell who you can trust.

Elektra, leader of the group of ninja assassins known as The Hand, was killed in battle with the New Avengers. However, it emerged that the being who seemed to be Elektra was actually a shapeshifting Skrull.

The New Avengers were shocked and wondered if any of their members might also be Skrulls.

Elektra
When Elektra died, her true identity was revealed. This Elektra was actually a Skrull.

The Skrulls are an alien race who are determined to invade Earth. They can change their appearance, which is known as shapeshifting.

They also worried that the Skrulls might be invading Earth.

Iron Man was the first of the New Avengers to be suspected of being a Skrull. Spider-Woman showed him the Skrull's body. If Iron Man was a Skrull, he would react to seeing another one. However, it was clear that Iron Man was not a Skrull.

When Tony showed the Skrull's body to the Illuminati, it was a different story. It revealed that Black Bolt was a Skrull. As the Skrull's secret invasion got more serious, the New Avengers teamed up with S.H.I.E.L.D. to put an end to it.

Shapeshifting
Using their abilities, the Skrulls can make themselves look like any individual they want.

Green Goblin
The Green Goblin flies on his Goblin Glider and tosses explosive pumpkin bombs on his enemies.

The Cabal
Emma Frost, Doctor Doom, Loki and the Hood joined Norman Osborn in the Cabal.

Dark reign

Iron Man was forced to step down as leader of S.H.I.E.L.D. and the Avengers because he failed to stop the Skrull's secret invasion.

He was replaced by Norman Osborn, Spider-Man's greatest enemy. Osborn joined with some powerful but evil allies and formed the secret society called the Cabal. Iron Man was now on the run.

No one knows what is next for Iron Man. Only time will tell if he will take his place again as one of the world's greatest Super Heroes.

Fugitive
After the secret invasion, the once-great hero became a wanted man.

Thinking time
Iron Man will need to work hard to win back people's trust and respect.

Glossary

aftermath
A period following an event.

ambassador
A representative of a government in another country.

android
A robot.

arsenal
A collection, usually of weapons.

boarding school
A private school where students live and study together.

butler
A male servant who takes care of all the needs of a household.

chauffeur
A person employed to drive a car.

commando
A member of a military unit.

cybernetic
Artificial or mechanical.

disassemble
To break apart.

donned
Put on.

embedded
Placed in.

espionage
To do with spying.

flexible
Easily bendable.

force field
A barrier made of energy to protect someone.

gamma ray
Radiation of high energy.

graduated
Having completed college with a degree.

gravitational pull
The power of Earth's gravity.

holograms
Three-dimensional images.

levitation
The act of rising or floating in the air.

manipulated
Controlled or influenced.

mistrusting
Not trusting.

mutant
A non-human who is born with special abilities.

registration
The act of listing or keeping records about something.

repulsor
Something that forces a thing back.

solar
To do with the sun.

staunchest
Strongest.

stock-car race
A race using cars that are similar to passenger cars.

sturdiest
The thing that is built the strongest.

thermal
To do with heat.

tornado
A violent windstorm.

uplifts
The act of raising something up.